Published by:
Bailiwick Press
309 East Mulberry Street
Fort Collins, Colorado 80524
www.bailiwickpress.com

Manufactured by:
Friesens Corporation
Altona, Canada
June 2019
Job # 256462

Book design by:
Launie Parry
Red Letter Creative
www.red-letter-creative.com

ISBN 978-1-934649-63-3

Printed in Canada

25 24 23 22 21 20 19

10 9 8 7

GOODNIGHT UNICORN

A Magical Parody

By Pearl E. Horne

Illustrated by Kendra Spanjer

BAILIWICK PRESS

In the great green wood,
there were sweet hawthorns,
and breezes warm,
and a blessing of...

...unicorns with spiraling horns.

And there were three little fairies sitting on cherries.

And two drowsy foals being read to by trolls.

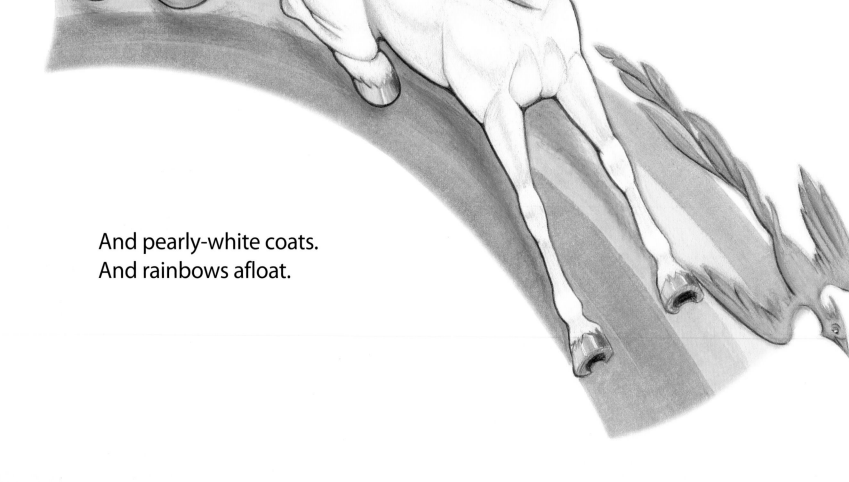

And pearly-white coats.
And rainbows afloat.

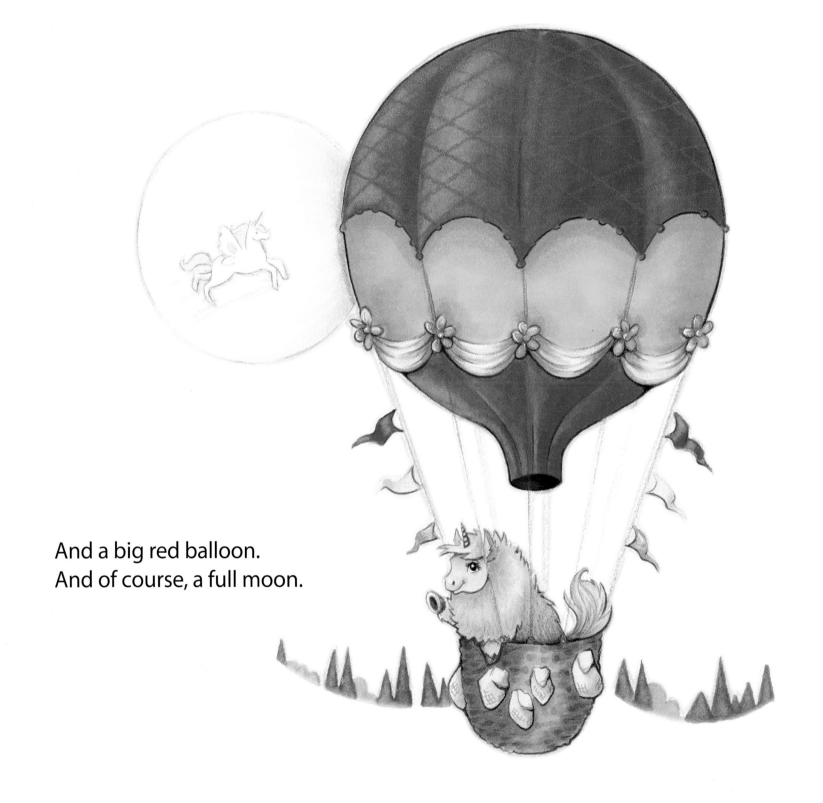

And a big red balloon.
And of course, a full moon.

And flowing silk manes. And nighttime refrains.

And a gnome with a brush. And a nuzzling blush.
And soft phoenix feathers that fall with a hush.

Goodnight unicorns. Goodnight horns.
Goodnight breeze and sweet hawthorns.

CRACK!

Goodnight fairies. Goodnight cherries.

Goodnight foals and goodnight trolls.

Goodnight olden. Goodnight beauty.

Goodnight cutie with tattooed patootie.

Goodnight purple. Goodnight pink.

Goodnight colts and bashful wink.

Goodnight rainbow. Goodnight jet black

Goodnight plum
and flutterback.

Goodnight mane and lashy eye.

Goodnight gnome and dragon fly.

Goodnight fluffy. Goodnight balloon.

Goodnight goodness. Goodnight moon.

Goodnight wonder beyond compare.

Goodnight
unicorn lovers
everywhere.

UNICORNOLOGY
Magical facts unicorn lovers love to know!

While a group of horses is called a herd, a group of unicorns is a "blessing." Unicorns live together in blessings made up of an elder, parents, and children.

Unicorn babies are born without horns. Their horns grow as they grow.

Unicorns are intelligent and good. Only people who are also pure of heart can see unicorns. To others they remain invisible or sometimes look like regular horses.

Sometimes unicorns enjoy eating plants and grains, just like horses, but their horns also absorb energy directly from the moon.

Rainbows and unicorns go together because both are pure, magical, and rarely seen up close. Unicorns can also use rainbows as slides.

Unicorns sleep on phoenix-feather beds, which are as soft as a whisper and float up into the air.

Unicorns are naturally gentle and kind, but if they need to defend themselves or their families and friends, they can be fierce warriors.

Unicorns live in forests with other woodland and magical creatures. Sweet-smelling hawthorn trees often mark the entrance to unicorn forests.

Unicorns live to be hundreds and even thousands of years old.

Unicorns communicate by reading minds. They can also speak if they wish. They know every language.

Some unicorns have wings and can fly. Pegasus is a famous flying horse, so flying unicorns are sometimes called "pegacorns" or "unipegs."

KNOW YOUR UNICORNS

The unicorn's spiraling horn is called an "alicorn." Alicorns grow to different lengths and can sparkle, change colors, and glow in the dark. They are also magic and heal anything they touch. Sometimes unicorns are born with smooth horns that don't spiral. **Can you find any smooth horns in this book?**

Male unicorns often have beards. **Which unicorns have beards in this book?**

Unicorns' coats may be white, black, or any color. They can also be patterned. **How many coat colors and patterns can you find in this book?**

Some unicorns have cloven hooves, like goats or deer. Others have hooves like horses. **Which unicorns have cloven hooves and which have horse-like hooves in this book?**

Unicorn eyelashes are long and lush. Most unicorns have blue or purple eyes, but sometimes their eyes are other colors. **Which eye colors do you see in this book?**

Grown-up unicorns usually have long, flowing manes and tails. Some have tails like lions. **Can you spot a unicorn with a lion-like tail in this book?**

Which unicorn is **your** favorite? **Why?**